The Big Race

Creepy Crawlies

Join the Creepy Crawlies in all their
fun-packed adventures!

 Be sure to read:

Home Sweet Home

The Talent Contest

Shop Till We Drop

The Big Race

Tony Bradman
illustrated by Damon Burnard

SCHOLASTIC

For Jane,
who never answers the phone

Scholastic Children's Books,
Commonwealth House, 1-19 New Oxford Street,
London, WC1A 1NU, UK
a division of Scholastic Ltd
London ~ New York ~ Toronto ~ Sydney ~ Auckland
Mexico City ~ New Delhi ~ Hong Kong

First published by Scholastic Ltd, 2005

Text copyright © Tony Bradman, 2005
Illustrations copyright © Damon Burnard, 2005

ISBN 0 439 95984 5

All rights reserved

Printed and bound by Tien Wah Press Pte. Ltd, Singapore

10 9 8 7 6 5 4 3 2 1

The rights of Tony Bradman and Damon Burnard to be identified as the
author and illustrator of this work respectively have been asserted by
them in accordance with the Copyright, Designs and Patents Act, 1988.

Chapter One

In a corner of The Garden, beyond The Flower Bed and underneath The Big Bush, four little friends were getting ready for another busy day.

Lucy the Ladybird was going to the library.

Imelda the Centipede was heading off to The Garden Mall to shop for shoes.

Doug the Slug was planning a sale of his old games and comics to raise some money.

And at three o'clock that afternoon …
Billy the Beetle was due to take
part in The Big Race at
The Garden Stadium.
He was keen to pop over
there during the
morning to check out the
track. He was very excited.

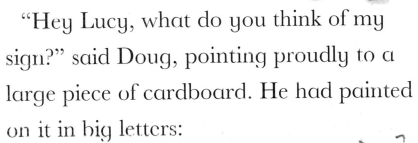

"Hey Lucy, what do you think of my
sign?" said Doug, pointing proudly to a
large piece of cardboard. He had painted
on it in big letters:

SALe
toDaY-
GReAt
baRGAiNS
-eveRything
Must GO!

"Very nice, Doug," said Lucy. "Just don't make a mess outside."

"And don't go in my room," said Imelda. "Or anywhere near it."

"Huh, don't do this, don't do that," Doug muttered. "Is there anything else I'm not allowed to do? I'll be glad when you two have gone!"

"Not half as glad as me," said Lucy. "I can't wait to have some time to myself. And how are you feeling, Billy? You need to stay calm."

"I'm trying to," said Billy. "But I'm pretty nervous, actually…"

"Don't be," said Lucy. "I'm sure you're going to win. And we'll be there to cheer you on, won't we?"

Imelda nodded, and Doug shrugged.

"Oh, and by the way, Billy," Lucy added. "I'm leaving you in charge."

"Because he's the sensible one," said Imelda, "and you're not."

"Shut up, stinky!" Doug snapped, and stuck his tongue out at her.

"Point proven, I think," said Lucy. "Billy, I'm counting on you to make sure Doug doesn't get up to any mischief."

Billy waved goodbye from the front door. Of course, it meant he wouldn't be able to go to The Garden Stadium this morning. But he was pleased Lucy had left him in charge. It made him feel quite grown up.

Little did he know what a terrible nightmare was about to unfold…

Chapter Two

Billy kept an eye on Doug as he set up his
stall outside the house. Doug tied the sign
to the hedge, put price tags on everything,
then … waited.

"Are you going to stand there watching me all morning, Billy?" he muttered. "You'll probably get trampled to death in the rush."

"Huh, as if," said Billy. "Anyway, I'm happier with you in my sight."

"Oh, come on," said Doug. "You don't seriously think I'm going to get up to anything much out here, do you?"

"Well, I suppose I ought to rest…" said Billy. "Okay then. But remember, I'll only be in the house – so I'll still be able to see what you're doing."

Billy went indoors.

It was ten o'clock.
He tried hard to relax,
but he felt very restless.

He looked at the sports pages of the *Garden News*.

He watched TV for a while.

Then he looked out of the window.

Doug was standing at his stall, but now he was talking to Wilma the Worm. It all looked innocent enough. "Umm, maybe I can slip away after all," Billy thought. He really, really wanted to go to The Garden Stadium…

He went outside again. Several eager young snails were sliding towards Doug's stall, and Dora the Dragonfly was hovering over it as well.

"I'm, er … off to run an errand, Doug," Billy said. "I'll be back soon."

"No problem, Billy," Doug said happily, taking money from Wilma.

Bye!

Billy arrived at the stadium a little while later. He walked round it, then slipped in through the entrance to look at the track and the rows of seats. The stadium was awesome even though it was empty, and Billy knew that in the afternoon it would be teeming with cheering creepy crawlies.

Billy did a bit of warming up on the track,

then he sat down, his head full of dreams.

Time slipped past...
Suddenly he glanced at his watch. It was eleven o'clock!

He had been away from the house for a lot longer than he had planned… He jumped up and hurried home as quickly as he could.

A strange sight greeted him there. Doug's stall was cleared of everything and tipped over, and the sign was hanging off the hedge. Doug himself was nowhere to be seen, and the front door was wide open.

Billy hurried inside, and for a second he
wondered if he was in the right place.
The hall had been
stripped bare …

and so had the kitchen and the front room.

Doug was sitting on the
stairs looking totally dazed.

"Er, hi, Billy," he said.
"I think I've done
something silly…"

Chapter Three

"What do you mean, you've sold the entire contents of the house?" said Billy. "I don't believe it!" But it was true, as Billy discovered when he checked upstairs. "Oh no, this can't be happening to me…" he moaned.

"I sold what I had, then loads more customers turned up," said Doug with a nervous giggle.

"So I, er … needed more stuff from the house to sell. Then this creepy crawly with a big van came by. He saw my sign and offered to buy everything that was left."

"And you let him?" said Billy, amazed. "But why?"

"It seemed like a good idea at the time," said Doug. "I even sold him the TV," he added, shaking his head. "Can you imagine? I sold the TV…"

"What was this creepy crawly's name?" said Billy.

"Er… Dodgy Dave the Dung Beetle, I think," answered Doug. "This is the money he gave me. Listen, do you think Lucy and Imelda will be cross when they get home?"

"Well, let me see," said Billy, counting the money. "You've sold Lucy's books, Imelda's clothes and shoes, and the furniture, all for the price of a meal at Garden Burgers. So no, I don't think they'll be cross." Doug looked relieved.

"THEY'LL GO BERSERK!" Billy yelled. "You're right," Doug moaned, the colour suddenly draining from his face. "What are we going to do?"

"WE?" squeaked Billy. "Hey, this is nothing to do with me."

"But you have to help me," Doug said, his face taking on a crafty look. "Lucy left you in charge. You're in just as much trouble as I am…"

Billy opened his mouth to speak … but then he closed it, and sagged. Doug was right. Billy knew he should never have left Doug on his own. Lucy was going to be so disappointed with him.

Unless of course he could sort out this whole mess before Lucy came home…

"I have to stay calm…" he murmured. "Okay Doug, here's what we'll do. Can you remember who your other, er … customers were?"

Massage!

Rub! Rub!

"I think so," said Doug. "What's your plan then, Billy?"

"It's simple," said Billy. "We're going to get everything back." At least he hoped they were… He glanced at his watch again. "Yikes, it's twelve o'clock already!" he squealed. "Come on, we haven't a moment to lose!"

Especially if he was still going to make it to The Big Race…

Chapter Four

Billy set off running and Doug followed
him, puffing and panting.

"Hey, slow down, Billy," said Doug. "I can't keep up. And I've just thought of something. Do I have to give back the money, too?"

"Of course you do, dummy!" said Billy. "The creepy crawlies you sold stuff to aren't going to hand it over to us for nothing, are they?"

"Okay, Mr Grumpy…" Doug said sulkily. "I was only asking."

Grrr…

They went round the houses of all the creepy crawlies Doug had sold things to, starting with Dora the Dragonfly and Wilma the Worm. Billy did the talking …

and he soon discovered it wasn't going to be easy.

A few creepy crawlies simply laughed and returned what they had bought.

But many more
had to be persuaded,
which took time, and
several were quite
nasty and didn't
want to give up
their bargains.

Billy did manage to get back most of
Lucy's books though, and most of Imelda's
clothes and shoes. Soon he and Doug were
staggering along with heaps of stuff. They
hurried home and dumped it in the hall.

"Hey, shouldn't we try and tidy up a bit?" said Doug. "I mean, Lucy won't be very happy if she sees this lot piled up here, will she?"

"But we haven't got anywhere to put it!" said Billy. "We need to get the furniture back from Dodgy Dave. Where did you say he lives?"

"I didn't, did I?" said Doug. "I'm not sure I even know… I think there was an address on the side of his van, but I don't really remember."

Billy glanced at his watch, groaned, and held his head. "Oh no, Lucy and Imelda will be home soon," he said. "It's one o'clock…"

"Great!" said Doug. "Time for lunch. I'm absolutely starving…"

Grrr…

He paused and looked at Billy, who was glaring fiercely at him.

"You won't be eating lunch ever again if you don't come up with that address pretty sharpish, Doug," Billy snarled. "I swear I'll…"

"Er … hang on," said Doug, gulping. "It's coming back to me…"

It seemed that Dodgy Dave lived on Dung Heap Drive. He had a big, rambling house, and a front yard full of what looked like old junk. Then Billy realized that some of that old junk was actually their furniture…

Dodgy Dave listened as Billy explained that Doug should never have sold their stuff to him, and asked nicely if they could have it all back.

"Sure, no problem," said Dodgy Dave. He was extremely smelly. "So long as you give me what I paid for it. Plus a bit extra for my trouble."

In fact, he wanted a lot extra … more than Doug had, anyway.

"Sorry," said Dodgy Dave. "No extra cash, no furniture."

And with that he slammed the door shut in their faces.

Chapter Five

"Oh no! We've had it!" Doug moaned, and started banging on the door in his panic. "Please, Mr Dave, give us all our stuff back, pretty please…"

"Stand aside, Doug," said Billy angrily.
"I'll have another try."
Billy pounded on the
door till Dodgy
Dave opened it.

Billy talked very fast, and persuaded Dave
to give them back *some* furniture, at least.
Billy handed over all of the money, and
Dave slammed the door once more.

"Let's get this lot home," said Billy. "Maybe Lucy and Imelda won't notice there's still some stuff missing. I'll just have to think of a way to come up with some more money… Hey, are you listening, Doug?"

"TV, my lovely TV," Doug was murmuring. He was hugging the TV set, and his eyes were glistening with tears. "I promise we'll never be parted again, not as long as I live… Sorry, Billy, did you say something?"

"Give me strength…" Billy muttered, and rolled his eyes. He got Doug moving at last, though, and soon they were staggering home under an even bigger heap of stuff.

They were just going up the lane that led to the little house … when Billy saw something that made him go quite pale.

Lucy and Imelda were walking up the path towards the front door.

Billy dropped what he was carrying and ran up the path behind them.

"STOP!" he yelled. "DON'T GO IN THERE!" But it was too late…

Lucy opened the door … and stood there looking utterly stunned.

"Hey, those are my clothes … and my shoes!" said Imelda. "And where's all the furniture gone? What have you two been doing?"

"Well?" said Lucy, turning to Billy, her face stern. Doug had also appeared by now. He looked utterly terrified, and hid behind Billy.

Billy tried to think of a story that would save them. But he couldn't.

"I'm really sorry, Lucy," he murmured at last. "It was all my fault…"

Well, I, we, er...

44

And then he told her everything. Lucy listened, then she asked some questions, mostly about Dodgy Dave, and Billy did his best to answer.

"Whoa," said Imelda, impressed. "That's so bad it's almost cool."

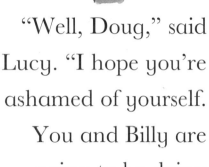

"Well, Doug," said Lucy. "I hope you're ashamed of yourself. You and Billy are going to be doing a lot of tidying up for the next few days."

"Ashamed?" said Doug, confused. "Oh, right. Yeah, of course."

"But you should also be grateful to Billy for trying to get you out of trouble," said Lucy. "You were silly to leave Doug, Billy, but at least you made an effort to sort things out. I think that was very grown up."

"You do?" squeaked Billy. "But what about Dodgy Dave and…"

"Oh, don't worry, I'll soon sort him out," said Lucy. "Now, don't you have a race to get ready for? We were coming to watch you, remember?"

Billy didn't need to be told twice, and ran off to get his stuff.

By the time Lucy had finished telling off Dodgy Dave it was nearly three o'clock – would they make it in time for The Big Race?

"We need a lift," said Lucy. "You'll take us to the stadium, Dodgy Dave – *won't you?* Unless you want me to have a word with the Garden Police..."

"He should be arrested just for wearing that vest," said Imelda.

"Er ... no problem," said Dodgy Dave. "Jump in..."

They climbed in his van and Dodgy Dave shot off.

They only just made it in time.

Billy quickly got changed ... lined up with the other competitors ... his friends cheered him on ... and he won, of course.

It felt like the second Big Race he'd been in that day, but he was still very happy. In fact ... they all were!